$1 \cdot 3 = 3$

$1 \cdot 4 = 4$

$1 \cdot 5 = 5$

$2 \cdot 2 = 4$

$2 \cdot 3 = 6$

$2 \cdot 4 = 8$

$3 \cdot 1 = 3$

$3 \cdot 2 = 6$

$3 \cdot 3 = 9$

$4 \cdot 3 = 12$

For Karianne

Text, cover, illustrations, and book design by Stian Hole

Translation by Don Bartlett

First published in Norway
© 2008 J.W. Cappelens Forlag

This edition published in 2010
by agreement with Cappelen by
Eerdmans Books for Young Readers
an imprint of Wm. B. Eerdmans Publishing Co.
2140 Oak Industrial Dr. NE, Grand Rapids, Michigan 49505
P.O. Box 163, Cambridge CB3 9PU U.K.

www.eerdmans.com/youngreaders

Manufactured at Millenium Litho Ltd., in Yangjiang, Guangdong, P.R. China,
December 2009, first printing

15 14 13 12 11 10   9 8 7 6 5 4 3 2 1

Text font Mrs. Eaves

This translation has been published
with the financial support of NORLA.

Library of Congress Cataloging-in-Publication Data
Hole, Stian.
[Garmanns gate. English]
Garmann's street / by Stian Hole ; translated by Don Bartlett.
p. cm.
Summary: After succumbing to peer pressure from a bully, an unusual
friendship between Garmann and the Stamp Man arises out of a near-disaster.
ISBN 978-0-8028-5357-8 (hardcover : alk. paper)
[1. Friendship--Fiction. 2. Bullies--Fiction. 3. Peer pressure--Fiction.]
I. Bartlett, Don. II. Title.
PZ7.H7072Gap 2010
[Fic]--dc22
                                    2009030388

Stian Hole

Garmann's Street

Eerdmans Books for Young Readers

Grand Rapids, Michigan • Cambridge, U.K.

From his window Garmann sees a black cat dash across the street. Seven years of bad luck, he thinks, as Roy from the fourth grade cycles past. Last year Roy threw his gym shoes up on the telephone wire. They are still hanging there.

Roy from the fourth grade says that the Stamp Man is a monster. That he kills kittens. "He puts them in a sack and drowns them in the bay at night," Roy says. Everyone listens to Roy even though he tells lies. On Garmann's street what Roy says goes. Roy is the president, the general, Congress, God, the basketball team's top scorer, and first in everything. Roy is *everything*, and his bike has 26 gears. The twins, Hannah and Johanna, blush and fall off the fence whenever Roy cycles past with no hands on the handlebars.

The Stamp Man is an old mailman who lives at the end of Garmann's street. His basement is full of letters and his head is full of ideas, neither of which have been sorted.

It's creepy going into the Stamp Man's overgrown yard. But as Daddy always says, "Life is never completely safe."

Walking into the Stamp Man's yard is like entering a dark forest or going down to the basement alone, thinks Garmann. But he has seen foxgloves and hound's-tongue, which he needs for his flower book for school.

So Garmann ventures in. Behind him he hears a deep voice.

I t is Roy, who has appeared from nowhere.
"You don't dare!" Roy says to Garmann.
"You little coward."

Roy puts a match into his hands. Garmann trembles,
frightened. He closes his eyes and wishes he were on
vacation in China or could disappear like the sparrows
in the hedge. The crows are sitting on the telephone
wires screaming warnings.

"Are you a wimp, Garmann? Are you too weak to light
a match?" Roy whispers in his ear. Garmann can
smell raspberry candy and feel Roy's hot
breath on his cheek. Garmann goes
hot and cold at the same time.

"Only those who are really frightened can
be brave," Daddy always says. But who can
be brave when Roy is blocking the gate?

Hedgehogs, badgers, and earwigs live in the high grass in the overgrown garden, thinks Garmann, striking the match against the box. His hands are shaking. The yellow and red flame moves slowly down, making the match go black.

It takes the flame at least seven years to reach his fingertips.

Garmann burns his finger and drops the match. It falls to the ground, but before he can do anything, the dry grass has caught fire.

Garmann stops breathing, the crows fall silent, and Roy goes pale. The burning grass smells sweet and sharp. The fire crackles and spreads like lightning. Soon the flames are everywhere, and the sparrows in the hedge take to the air.

"You did that!" Roy says and is gone.

Garmann cries. He stamps on the burning grass as the flames spread around his legs. The smoke makes his eyes sting. He takes off his T-shirt and whirls it around to put out the flames. He wants to shout for help, but his tongue is dry and large and sticks to the roof of his mouth, and all the words catch in his throat.

he Stamp Man has seen everything from his kitchen window and now he rushes out shrieking. He grabs the hose and turns on the water. "Run and get help!" he shouts to Garmann. And Garmann runs home. He runs across the street without looking. He feels as if he has lead in his shoes. His whole body aches and his stomach is tied in knots.

He can hear his mother calling him from far away.

eighbors run over with buckets of water. Then there are sirens, distant at first, but getting closer and closer. Mama takes Garmann's hand and they hurry back to help.

It doesn't take the firefighters long to put out the burning grass.

Afterward Garmann's burns are treated with cold water and a bandage. "Seven calls today! It's a shame God turned off the water before going on vacation," Garmann hears a fireman say to one of the adults as he drags the hoses back over the scorched ground.

At least you didn't scamper off," the Stamp Man whispers to Garmann when everything is over and all the neighbors have gone home. Garmann looks down at the ground. The old man puts the matches in his pocket without Mama seeing. Garmann is sweaty and dirty, and his mind goes blank.

The Stamp Man goes inside and locks the door.

In the next few days Garmann saunters slowly past the Stamp Man's house. Through the kitchen window he can see the old man behind the curtains. Then one afternoon, when the mailman is sitting outside on the steps, Garmann ventures through the gate again. He has his flower book with him. Daddy has helped him spell the long names — *germander speedwell, bloody cranesbill,* and *hairy rock cress.* They have pressed and dried the flowers in the last volume of the encyclopedia, between the letters of x, y, and z.

The Stamp Man flicks through the flower book with interest. He takes his time, for he has no work to do.

Behind his house there are several flowers Garmann does not have in his collection. "Agrimony, viper's bugloss, and eyebright," the Stamp Man says, passing the flowers to Garmann. He does not mention the fire. As Garmann leaves, the old man gives him a handful of stamps from countries Garmann has never heard of.

On the way home, Garmann practices his whistling.

Who are all the letters for?" Garmann asks one afternoon. Now he is not afraid of going in the gate and across the scorched lawn.

The Stamp Man smiles and lifts the cat onto his lap. It purrs when he scratches it behind the ears. "We're both collectors, Garmann," he chuckles, but says nothing about the letters. Just: "They've been lying around for years. Not all letters reach their destinations."

"If you live to be a hundred, you'll get a letter from the president," Garmann replies.

 "**I**n China they are building a dam which is so big that the earth's center of gravity will shift and the world will spin unevenly on its axis," the Stamp Man says one afternoon, rolling his eyes. "We'll be thrown off as it rotates," he whispers, eating a piece of licorice. Garmann tries not to look at the shiny dewdrop hanging from the tip of his nose.

"We'll definitely get very dizzy," Garmann says, and produces a perfect whistled note.

In the evening Garmann puts all of his stamps in the large matchbox he keeps with his flower book under his bed. When his mother straightens the covers over him and strokes his cheek, he thinks about the big dam.

"One human year is seven dog years, a cat has nine lives, and humans consist of 73% water," the Stamp Man says the next time they are sitting on the steps with the flower book. "You think 50,000 thoughts every day!" He is good with numbers. He knows all the zip codes from Holtsville 00501 to Ketchikan 99950. "If you stretch out your intestines, they will be over twenty-five feet long. Everything can be divided by two, but some things you have to do alone," he says with a sly smile.

Garmann whistles to the cat. "There are 440 steps to school, 230 days until summer vacation, 366 days in a leap year, and I am always last to be picked when we make teams at recess time," Garmann answers. He likes arithmetic too, even though he finds times tables hard.

"There are always some calculations that don't work," the Stamp Man says, wiping the dewdrop with the back of his hand.

"Research has shown that you will meet about 200,000 people in the course of the 30,000 days you can hope to live," the Stamp Man explains one day when they are sitting at the kitchen table. "That's 3.5 billion heartbeats," he says in a low voice, slurping from his cup of coffee. At last it has begun to rain outside. It is pouring down, and the pavement is covered with wet leaves and white worm trails.

"I think I've met almost everyone now," he adds. "I'm happy I managed to meet you."

On the way home Garmann thinks about all the people he has yet to meet. He looks up and whistles at the gym shoes on the telephone wire.

It is late autumn, and Garmann's street is quiet, apart from the crows gathering in the park and the leaf blower collecting all the brown leaves in one big heap. Nothing grows anymore.

The leaf blower is like a creature from another galaxy, thinks Garmann.

R oy from the fourth grade crouches over his bike and cycles past the Stamp Man's house. Roy has started to hold the handlebars now, and the twins don't fall off the fence when he passes anymore.

Garmann can see everything from his window.